P9-DDU-880

This book
belongs to:

_____

MESSAGE TO PARENTS

This book is perfect for parents and children to read aloud together. First read the story to your child. When you read it again, run your finger under each line, stopping at each picture for your child to "read." Help your child to figure out the picture. If your child makes a mistake, be encouraging as you say the right word. Point out the written word beneath each picture in the margin on the page. Soon your child will be "reading" aloud with you, and at the same time learning the symbols that stand for words.

Library of Congress Cataloging-in-Publication Data

Meltzer, Lisa.
    The three billy goats Gruff / retold by Lisa Meltzer ; illustrated by Heidi Petach.
        p.   cm. — (A Read along with me book)
    Summary: A rebus version of the fairy tale in which three clever billy goats outwit a big, ugly troll living under the bridge they wish to cross.
    ISBN 0-02-898242-8
    [1. Fairy tales.   2. Folklore—Norway.   3. Rebuses.] I. Petach, Heidi, ill.   II. Asbjørnsen, Peter Christen, 1812–1885. Tre bukkene Bruse. III. Title. IV. Series.
PZ8.M5217Th   1989
398.2'45297358'09481—dc19
[E]   89-591
                                                                                 CIP
                                                                                  AC

The Three Billy Goats Gruff

A Read Along With Me Book

Retold by **Lisa Meltzer**
Illustrated by **Heidi Petach**

CHECKERBOARD PRESS
NEW YORK

hill

three

goats

grass

river

Once on the side of a big

there lived billy . All

 were named Gruff. They

lived very happily eating the

sweet green on the

beside a .

One day the smallest billy looked at the on the other side of the and said, "That

 is prettier than ours. The

 is greener, and I am sure

it is sweeter, too." So the little

billy set off across the

over the  to the where

the was green and sweet.

Now, under the lived the

ugliest and meanest

goat

bridge

troll

bridge

goat

troll

anybody had ever seen. No one

could cross the without

his say-so. But trip-trap, trip-trap,

over the went the little

billy  Gruff.

"Who is that trip-trapping over

my ?" roared the ugly

in his ugly  voice.

"Oh, just me, Little Billy

Gruff," said the little billy  in

his little billy  voice.

"I am going across the to eat the sweet green on the pretty ."

"Well," said the ugly in his ugly voice, "I am going to eat YOU!" And he climbed up onto the .

grass

hill

goat

troll

bridge

"No, no!" said the little billy . "I am much too small and thin. Why not wait for my brother Billy  Gruff. He will be along soon. He is much bigger than I am. Then you will have more to eat."

"Well, all right," said the .

So trip-trap, trip-trap, across the went Little Billy Gruff. And the sat down and waited for the next billy .

goat

troll

bridge

grass

"No, no!" said the second billy . "I am too thin. There is hardly any fat on me. Why not wait for my brother Big Billy Gruff. He will be along soon. He is much bigger than I am. Then you will have more to eat."

"Well, all right," said the . So trip-trap, trip-trap, across the  went the second billy Gruff. And the went back

The did not have long to wait. When the second billy Gruff saw the little billy eating the sweet green he said, "My little brother is right.

hill

grass

bridge

troll

That is prettier than ours.

The is greener, and I am

sure it is sweeter."

So trip-trap, trip-trap, across the

 he went. But when the ugly

 heard his steps he said

in his ugly voice, "Who is

that trip-trapping over my ?"

"Oh, just me, Billy 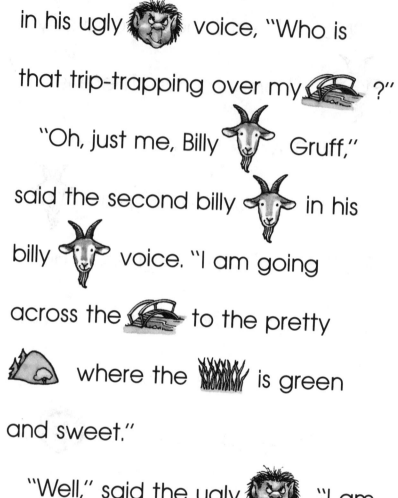 Gruff,"

said the second billy 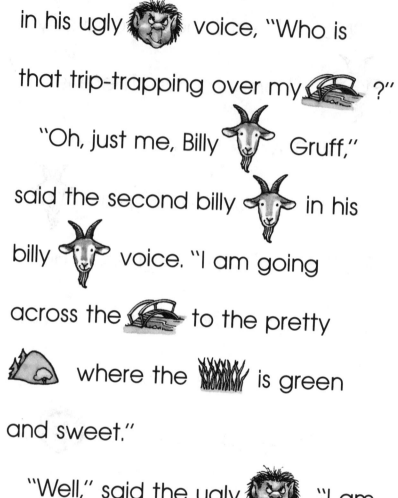 in his

billy 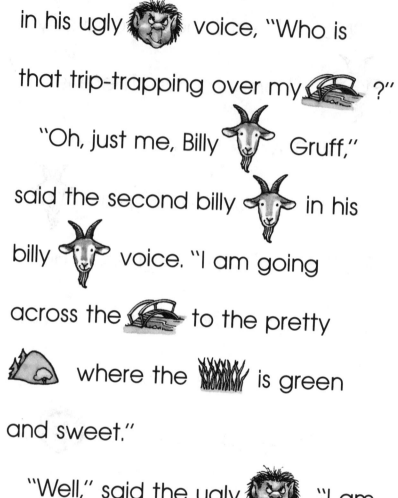 voice. "I am going

across the to the pretty

 where the is green

and sweet."

"Well," said the ugly , "I am

going to eat YOU!" And he

climbed up onto the .

goat

and sat down under the  to

wait for the next billy  Gruff.

Again, the  did not have

long to wait.

goat

goats

grass

hill

When the big billy

Gruff saw the other billy

Gruff eating the sweet green

 he said, "I think my brothers

are right. That is prettier

than ours. The  is greener,

and I am sure it is sweeter."

So trip-trap, trip-trap, across

the he went. But when

the heard the big billy

Gruff on the  he said,

bridge

goat

"Who is that trip-trapping over my ?"

"Oh, just me, Big Billy Gruff," said the big billy Gruff in his big billy voice. "I am going across the to the

pretty where the is

sweet and green."

"Well," said the ugly in

his ugly voice, "I am going

to eat YOU!" And he climbed up

onto the .

hill

grass

troll

goat

troll

bridge

"Oh, you are, are you?" said

the big billy  Gruff. He

lowered his head, and with his

great big horns he butted

the right off the !

No one has seen the ugly

since that day. And whenever

the billy Gruff want to

eat the sweet green on the

pretty on the other side of

the , off they go across the

 , trip-trap, trip-trap, trip-trap.

three

goats

grass

hill

river

Words I can read

- ☐ bridge
- ☐ goat
- ☐ goats
- ☐ grass
- ☐ hill
- ☐ river
- ☐ three
- ☐ troll